kratts' CREATURES™

WHERE'RE THE BEARS?

**By Martin Kratt
and Chris Kratt**

SCHOLASTIC INC.

New York   Toronto   London   Auckland   Sydney

To Laura

Exclusive worldwide licensing agent: Momentum Partners, Inc., NY
Photo credits:
Front Cover: (bear photo) © Steven Walker; (other photos) © 1997 Paragon Entertainment Corporation
Back Cover: (top) © Tom McHugh/Photo Researchers, Inc.; (bottom left and right) © 1997 Paragon Entertainment Corporation; **p. 3** Laura Wilkinson/© 1997 Paragon Entertainment Corporation; **p. 4** © R. Van Nostrand/Photo Researchers, Inc. **p. 5** (left) © Tom and Pat Leeson/Photo Researchers, Inc.; (right) © Tom McHugh/Photo Researchers, Inc. **p. 6** (left) © 1997 Paragon Entertainment Corporation; (right) © Natural History Museum, London **p. 7** painting by David Kirscher/© Weldon Owen Publishing **p. 8** illustration by Barbara P. Moore **p. 9** Laura Wilkinson/© 1997 Paragon Entertainment Corporation **p. 10** (left) Laura Wilkinson/ © 1997 Paragon Entertainment Corporation; (right) © Jeff Lepore/Photo Researchers, Inc. **p. 11** (all photos) Laura Wilkinson/ © 1997 Paragon Entertainment Corporation **p. 12** Eric Robertson © 1997 Paragon Entertainment Corporation **p. 13** (left) © Lynn Rogers/Peter Arnold, Inc.; (right) Laura Wilkinson/ © 1997 Paragon Entertainment Corporation **p. 14** © Thomas D. Mangelsen/Peter Arnold, Inc. **p. 15** (left) © Wayne Lankinen/DRK Photo; (right) Laura Wilkinson/ © 1997 Paragon Entertainment Corporation **p. 16** © Mark Newman/Earth Images **p. 17** (left) © Gary Milburn/Tom Stack & Associates; (right) painting by David Kirscher/ © Weldon Owen Publishing **p. 18** © Wardene Weisser/Bruce Coleman Inc. **p. 19** Anthony Mercieca Photo/Photo Researchers, Inc. **p. 20** © Terry Domico/Earth Images **p. 21** (left) © R. Van Nostrand/Photo Researchers, Inc.; (right) Laura Wilkinson/ © 1997 Paragon Entertainment Corporation **p. 22** © Tom and Pat Leeson/Photo Researchers, Inc. **p. 23** (right) © Mark Newman/Earth Images; (left) © Roy Morsch/Bruce Coleman Inc. **p. 24** © Mark Newman/Earth Images **p. 25** (top) © Tom McHugh/Photo Researchers, Inc.; (middle) © Jany Sauvanet/Photo Researchers, Inc.; (bottom) © 1997 Paragon Entertainment Corporation **p. 26** © 1997 Paragon Entertainment Corporation **p. 28** (left) Laura Wilkinson/ © 1997 Paragon Entertainment Corporation; (right) © Joel Bennett/Peter Arnold, Inc. **p. 29** (left) © Thomas D. Mangelsen/Peter Arnold, Inc.; (right) E & P Bauer/Bruce Coleman Inc. **p. 30** (clockwise) © Tom McHugh/Photo Researchers, Inc.; © Dieter & Mary Plage/Bruce Coleman Inc.; © C & M Denis-Huot/Peter Arnold, Inc.; © 1997 Paragon Entertainment Corporation; © Tim Davis/Photo Researchers, Inc. **p. 31** (left) Laura Wilkinson/ © 1997 Paragon Entertainment Corporation; (right) © Mark Newman/Earth Images **p. 32** Laura Wilkinson/ © 1997 Paragon Entertainment Corporation.

ISBN 0-590-06740-0

Book design by Todd Lefelt

10 9 8 7 6 5 4 3 2 1   7 8 9/9 0 1 2/0

Printed in the U.S.A.   24
First Scholastic printing, October 1997

3

You can find bears all over the world.

North America

Eurasia

Africa

South America

Australia

Antarctica

They're just about everywhere —
except a few places like Antarctica,
Australia, and Africa.

We can understand why there aren't
any bears in Antarctica because this
continent is an island that's far out
to sea. A bear would have to swim
hundreds of miles to get there. That's
just too far for a bear to swim.

Australia is another big island that bears can't get to, either. Of course, koala bears don't count. Koala bears aren't really bears. Koalas are related to kangaroos!

But bears could get to Africa. A brown bear from Eurasia could walk south to Africa and then splash up the Nile River until it wandered onto the African savanna. And the African savanna should be a fantastic place for a bear to live. It has a good climate with tons of food, but no bears! Why not?

"Why aren't there any bears in Africa?"

That's what we've got to find out!

Hey, guys, Allison here at the Creature Club! Here's some prehistory on bears to get us started on our search!

Agriotherium

A long, long time ago (five million years ago to be exact), a bear called *Agriotherium* (ag-ree-o-theer-ee-um) did live in Africa, but only for a very short time. We don't know much about it, or what happened to it, but check out this other prehistoric bear....

THE GIANT SHORT-FACED BEAR!

The giant short-faced bear was the largest bear that ever lived! It was *twice* as large as any living bear. Scientists think it had such long legs because it chased woolly mammoths, giant buffalo, and other big prey across the plains of North America. The giant short-faced bear became extinct about 12,000 years ago, when the big creatures it ate disappeared. As far as we know, giant short-faced bears never lived in Africa.

Okay, so let's look at the bears from around the world that are still alive. Maybe we can find some clues as to why there aren't any bears in Africa today.

Sun Bear

Moon Bear

Spectacled Bear

Panda Bear

Sloth Bear

Black Bear

Polar Bear

Brown (Grizzly) Bear

**There are eight bear species.
Let's visit these bears and figure this out!
First stop, North America!**

I can't *bear* the smell! But I have found a clue. It's a poo clue – a sure sign that a bear's been here!

And from the looks of it, you can even see the seeds of some berries it's been eating.

It's a blackberry patch, and bears love berries of all kinds.

They pluck the berries off with their lips.

But how do they deal with the thorns? Bears have very tough lips. One thing's for sure — bears are much better berry pickers than I am.

Bears are much better tree climbers, too.
Make way for our first bear...

THE AMERICAN BLACK BEAR!

Whoa! I *bearly* made it up the tree in time!

WARNING — Bears can be dangerous. In this picture, Chris is way too close for comfort. Always give wild bears a lot of room.

The black bear lives in the swamps, forests, and deserts of North America. Black bears eat anything from berries to rabbits to bugs. So they're called *omnivores* — which means they'll eat just about anything! There are more American black bears than any other kind of bear in the world! But for some reason, none of them live in Africa. **Hmmmmm...**

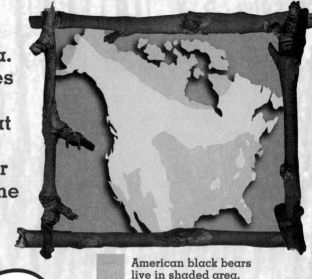

American black bears live in shaded area.

Hey, Martin— what bear is the opposite of the black bear?

I know who you're talking about, Chris. Let's head farther north and meet...

THE POLAR BEAR

Polar bears live in the lands of ice and snow that surround the North Pole. A polar bear hunts birds, rabbits, seals, and even walruses. He sneaks up on these animals by blending into the white snow. He even puts a paw over his black nose so he can hide completely. But even a polar bear occasionally likes to eat his vegetables — seaweed. Yuck.

Polar bears are the biggest of all living bears. When a polar bear stands on his hind feet, he's as tall as two people!

Whoaahhh!

Owww! Your boots are killing me! Why didn't you go *bear* foot?

Polar bears live in the shaded area.

It's easy to figure out why polar bears don't live in Africa. They couldn't take the heat! However, if you travel south from the North Pole for about 10,800 miles, you might bump into the spectacular ...

SPECTACLED BEAR

The spectacled bear is the only bear that lives in South America. These shy bears live high in the cloud forests of the Andes Mountains. Spectacled bears are great tree climbers — probably the best of all the bears! When a spectacled bear eats in a fruit tree, she builds a feeding platform by bending branches together!

Very little is known about spectacled bears, but we do know that they are closely related to the giant short-faced bear.

Spectacled bears live in the shaded area.

You can see it in the shape of the face. Here's another little piece of bear trivia. The spectacled bear is the only bear in the world with 13 pairs of ribs. All other bears have 14.
Do you know how many pairs of ribs humans have?

To find another shy bear of the mountains, we have to go to the other side of the world, to Asia. There we'll meet the only other bear that lives south of the equator....

17

Humans have 12 pairs of ribs.

THE SUN BEAR

Sun bears live in the shaded area.

The sun bear lives in the rain forests of Southeast Asia. He is the rarest and most mysterious of all the bears. He's also the smallest bear in the world. But like all the others, the sun bear has what it takes to be a bear.

The Bear Necessities

Eyes that see things sharply up close and also see movement far away.

Good nose for finding food.

Mouth that swallows plants and animals.

Sharp Claws for digging, catching fish, fighting, ripping up logs.

Strong arms for climbing.

Strong legs for running—sometimes as fast as a horse.

One special thing about the sun bear is that of all the bears in the world, it's the best at finding honey! In fact, that long tongue is specially designed for slurping it up!

Bears have an all-around athletic body designed for eating a variety of foods and living in a range of places — but why not Africa? We're still not sure, but we do know who the sun bear's neigh*bear* is...

THE ASIATIC BLACK BEAR

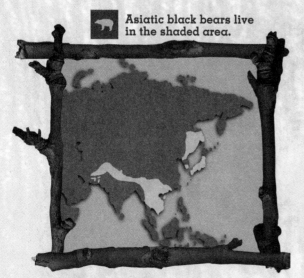

Asiatic black bears live in the shaded area.

Also called the "Moon Bear of Tibet" because of the white moon shape on its chest, this bear lives in some of the same forests as the sun bear — but the moon bear doesn't live south of the equator.

The moon bear eats a lot of fruits and nuts. But a moon bear doesn't wait for the fruits and nuts to fall; she climbs up trees after them. Because she climbs so much, a moon bear has especially strong front legs.

In fact, a moon bear is so strong, she could turn over a huge boulder with a single paw!

UGHHH. Turning over a boulder like this really is a *bear* of a job.

That was weak, Martin.

Tell me about it – we haven't even budged this thing!

No, I mean the joke.

Oh... sorry.

Bears are strong, but are they tough enough to survive in Africa? For one thing, moon bears are sometimes killed by leopards. Would any bear be able to fight off a pride of lions?

That would be tough, especially for the next bear who is just a peaceful plant eater...

21

THE GIANT PANDA BEAR

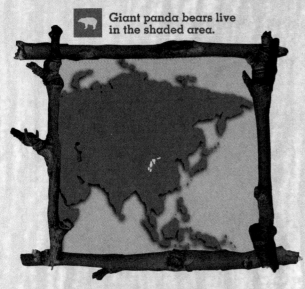

Giant panda bears live in the shaded area.

Giant pandas live in the mountain forests of China. They are very rare and have a very special diet. Giant pandas eat a lot of bamboo. Since they can live only where a lot of bamboo is growing, it makes sense that giant pandas don't live on the grasslands of Africa, where there is no bamboo.

Speaking of pandas, have you ever heard of the red panda? Some scientists think this red-furred, ring-tailed bamboo eater belongs in the bear family and others think it belongs in the raccoon family. What do you think?

Red Panda

Raccoon

Wait a second, we're getting sidetracked by another creature mystery! We still have to figure out why there aren't any bears in Africa. Let's meet our next type of bear...

THE SLOTH BEAR

Sloth bears live in shaded area.

Check out the weird hairdo!
Talk about an unusual bear.

The sloth bear roams around
India and is very unusual.

A sloth bear is missing his two upper front teeth. His lower lip is long, loose, and flexible. Together these creature features help a sloth bear eat his favorite food — termites! A sloth bear's lip can be used as a tube to suck up termites like a built-in straw! The termites zip right through the space between the bear's teeth and right into his mouth! Wow!

Did you know that scientists first thought this bear was a type of sloth and not a bear at all because of the way it hangs in trees? That's why they named it the sloth bear.

I'd rather call him Old Suction Face. He doesn't look like a sloth at all. Give me a *beark!*

You give me a break, Chris – that's not even a pun. You're em*bear*assing our whole family. Now *that's* a good one.

Sloth

It's not a bear like the bears on Earth, of course. The Great Bear is a constellation of stars that are in the rough shape of a bear. In fact, most people have seen this constellation because the Big Dipper is a part of it!

Earth to Al! We still have the last species of bear to check out down here.

THE BROWN BEAR

Brown bears live in the shaded area.

Anytime is bathtime for the brown bears!

A brown bear lives on the grasslands and in the forests of the northern hemisphere.

Brown bears love the water and are great at fishing!

Browns bears are often called other names, depending upon where they live. In most of the USA, they're called grizzly bears.

One time, when we were in Alaska, we saw a grizzly bear mom with two cubs. They were all playing and the mom was rolling the cubs around as if they were bowling balls!

The brown bear gobbles grass, catches fish, hunts deer and caribou, and is big and tough enough to stand up to a pack of wolves. Of all the bears alive today, a brown bear could probably do the best on the African savanna. In fact, a small group of brown bears once lived in northwestern Africa, but for some reason, they never could move south to the African savanna.

Hey, maybe the competition for food is so fierce down there that even a brown bear couldn't muscle his way in!

aardvark

mongoose

honey badger

hippo

Lions eat zebra.

Hyenas eat wildebeest.

Wild dogs eat antelope.

Crocodiles eat fish.

Honey badgers eat honey.

Mongooses eat beetles and other bugs.

Zebra, wildebeest, hippos, and antelope eat grass.

Baboons eat fruit, nuts, and berries.

Giraffes eat leaves.

Aardvarks eat ants and termites.

And more!

That's it!!!

...that are already eating what the brown bears would eat.

There are so many creatures in Africa ...

I think we've got a theory!

Let's call it **SUPER·OMNIVORIC** Competition.

We think that brown bears just haven't been able to move into Africa. Animals that already live there are so good at finding food that newly arriving brown bears couldn't find enough food to survive and get set up down there. The plant eaters are already eating all the plants; the hunters are eating all the prey. The brown bears, who eat a little bit of everything, would be left with the scraps. On top of that, super-predators like lions, hyenas, wild dogs, and leopards would all do their best to run the bears off the savanna.

But, of course, a theory is just a theory until you prove it.

So now we have to go to Africa and gather more information.

Let's go!

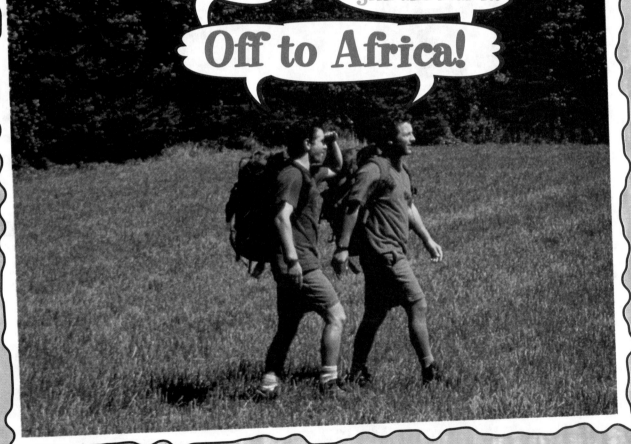